Just a Joke!

igloo

Little Monkey lives in the sprawly, crawly jungle.

He loves swinging by his tail and eating bananas.

He loves playing with his friends.

But when Little Monkey gets bored, he plays naughty tricks!

First, Snake hears Little Monkey calling for help.
"HELP! HELP!"
"Little Monkey is in trouble!" cries Snake.

Snake goes **HISS HISS HISSING** to the rescue.

But Little Monkey is playing tricks!
"BOO!" He leaps out of the hollow tree!
Snake jumps so much that she ties herself into a knot!

"Little Monkey, you're a pest!" hisses Snake, crossly.

"It's just a joke!" Little Monkey giggles.

Next, Lion Cub hears Little Monkey's voice.
"HELP! HELP!"
"Little Monkey is in trouble!" cries Lion Cub.

He goes **BOUND BOUND BOUNDING** to the rescue.

But Little Monkey is playing tricks!
Lion Cub bounds into a pile of prickles.

"Little Monkey, you're a **nuisance!**" Lion Cub roars.

"It's just a joke!" Little Monkey giggles.

Baby Hippo hears Little Monkey down by the river.
"HELP! HELP!"
"Little Monkey is in trouble!" cries Baby Hippo.

She goes **SPLOSH SPLOSH SPLOSHING** to the rescue.

But Little Monkey is playing tricks!
He throws squashy fruit at Baby Hippo's nose!
"Little Monkey, you're a **menace!**" bellows Baby Hippo.

"It's just a joke!" Little Monkey giggles.

Little Monkey plays tricks on **everyone**.

He creeps up on Crocodile. . .

. . .he ambushes Armadilo. . .

...and he ties some tangly twigs to Little Tiger's tail.

Little Monkey's friends meet by the long, yellow grass.

"I've had enough of Little Monkey's tricks!" says Snake.

"I don't want to play with him any more!" says Lion Cub.

"He's not my friend," says Baby Hippo.

Then they hear Little Monkey's voice.

"HELP! HELP! I'M STUCK IN THE MUD!"

"He's playing tricks again!" says Crocodile.
"I'm not falling for his jokes any more!"
says Armadillo.

But this time Little Monkey really **is** in trouble!

Poor Little Monkey waits and waits for his friends.

But nobody comes.

"Why don't they help me?" Little Monkey sobs.
"How will I ever get out?"

Then he hears a voice.

"Little Monkey! Where are you?"

She pulls Little Monkey out of the mud.

She wipes his muddy fur and washes him clean.

"None of my friends came to help me!" sniffs Little Monkey, sadly.

"You play too many tricks," says his mother.
"They don't know when to believe you."

"What if they don't want to be my friends
any more?" says Little Monkey.

"Don't be scared," his mother says.
"They will be your friends
if you say sorry."

Little Monkey finds his friends playing by the river.
"I'm sorry I played tricks on you," he cries.

"I promise, I will never play naughty tricks again!
Please, will you forgive me and be my friends?"

Little Monkey's friends gather around him.
They hug him and smile and laugh.
"Of course we forgive you, Little Monkey!" they shout.
"We're your friends forever!"

But Little Monkey's friends have their own trick to play!